Henry and Melinda
Sports Stories

HENRY AND MELINDA

By Silky Sullivan

Illustrations by Lois Axeman

 CHILDRENS PRESS, CHICAGO

For the real Henry and Linda

Library of Congress Cataloging in Publication Data

Sullivan, Silky.
  Henry and Melinda.

  (Henry and Melinda sports stories)
  Summary: Henry thinks that his sister
Melinda is too small to play ball with him,
but when he changes his attitude he's in for
a surprise.
  [1. Brothers and sisters—Fiction.
2. Baseball—Fiction] I. Axeman, Lois, ill.
II. Title. III. Series: Sullivan, Silky.
Henry and Melinda sports stories.
PZ7.S9537Hd   [Fic]   81-12283
ISBN 0-516-01916-3   AACR2

More than anything else, Henry loved to
play ball. He had a baseball and a bat.
He had a basketball and a net. He had
everything he needed except another player.

There were no other boys on the block.
There was only his little sister, Melinda.
She followed him everywhere. "Play with me,
Henry, play with me!"

This drove Henry wild.

"I don't want to play with you. I
baby-sit with you. Leave me alone."

Mother was on her way to work.
"Now, Henry, be nice," she said.
"Teach Melinda to play ball."
Then she went to work.

Henry glared.

"You don't know how to play ball," he
said. "You are too little to play ball.
You will get hurt playing ball. And you
will cry."

He threw the ball, hard.

"Catch!" he said.

Whap! Melinda went tumbling head over heels.

"See?" said Henry. "I said it would hurt."

Melinda got up. "Throw it again. I will catch it next time."

Henry was surprised. He threw it again.

Whap! Melinda went tumbling head over
heels.

"See?" said Henry. "You are too little."

Melinda got up. "I almost caught it.
I'm getting better."

Henry scratched his head. He threw
it again.

Whap! Again Melinda went tumbling head
over heels.

"See?" said Henry. "You will never
catch it."

Melinda got up. She looked puzzled.
"I thought playing ball would be fun," she said.
Henry turned red. "It *is* fun."

Melinda gave him the ball. "I think I will play something else," she said. "Something fun." She put her doll in the buggy.

Henry said, "Wait a minute. Nothing
is more fun than ball."

"Then, play," said Melinda.

"I don't have anyone to play with," said
Henry. An odd look came on his face.

"Hey, Mel," he said, "I really can teach you to play ball. I wasn't trying, before."

"No, thank you," said Melinda.

He followed her. "But, Mel, it was my fault you couldn't catch the ball. I threw it too hard on purpose."

"Is that so?" said Melinda.

Henry gave her the glove. He put the doll behind his back. "Come on, Mel. Play ball. I want you to like it as much as I do."

Melinda hid her smile. "Okay," she said.

This time Henry did not throw hard. The
ball went up. The ball came down. It
landed right in Melinda's glove.

Melinda was amazed. She fell flat on
her face.

Henry came running. "Melinda, speak to me!"
Melinda sat up. On her face was a smile.
In her glove was the ball. "That was fun,"
she said.

Henry jumped up and down. "You caught it,
Mel! You caught it! Now, we can really
play ball!"

The rest of the morning, they did just that.

They pitched.

They batted.

They slid into third. "Safe!" cried Henry. "Isn't this fun?"

Melinda was covered with Band-Aids and bruises. But she played on. Henry was proud of her.

"You learn fast," he said. "I must be a good teacher." He bought ice cream cones.

"Next, we will play basketball."

They did. Henry taught Melinda to dribble.
She dribbled with her left hand. She
dribbled with her right.

He taught her to pass.
Bounce. Pass. Bounce. Pass.
He taught her to shoot.
Hook shot. Jump shot. Lay-up.

They played one-on-one. Melinda played
hard. "Hey," said Henry, "I didn't teach
you all that stuff so you could beat me."
"I want to win," said Melinda.

When Mother came home, she asked, "What did you do today?"

"We played ball," said Henry. "Watch this."

Mother was delighted. "That calls for pancakes," she said.

She went in to start supper.

Henry said, "Just think, Mel! We can play ball all summer long. Won't that be fun?"

"You bet," said Melinda. "Pancakes every day!"

Unfamiliar Words
(based on the Spache Readability Formula)

Most of the following unfamiliar words in *Henry and Melinda*
are made clear through the illustrations and content.

amazed	doll	odd
Band-Aids	dribble	okay
baseball	dribbled	pancakes
basketball	everywhere	pitched
bat	fault	purpose
batted	glared	puzzled
bet	glove	stuff
bounce	heels	taught
bruises	hey	tumbling
buggy	hook	wasn't
cones	isn't	whap
couldn't	net	wild
delighted		

About the Author

Silky Sullivan is a Phi Beta Kappa graduate of the University of Michigan and a children's librarian who resides in Royal Oak, Michigan, with her artist husband and their tailless cat. The Henry and Melinda stories were inspired by her husband, who, at age fifteen, began teaching his younger sister, then three, to play basketball. His sister went on to become a superstar and very successful coach. Says Ms. Sullivan, "The whole family loves sports. We're all athletic. I'm writing from experience."

About the Artist

Lois Axeman is a native Chicagoan who lives with her Shih-tzu dog, Marty, in a sunny, plant-filled highrise overlooking a large Chicago park. Marty accompanies Lois to and from her studio in town. After attending the American Academy and the Institute of Design (IIT), Lois started as a fashion illustrator in a department store. When the children's wear illustrator became ill, Lois took her place and found that she loved drawing children. She started freelancing then, and has been doing text and picture books ever since. Lois teaches classes on illustration at the University of Illinois, Circle Campus.